ALPHA'S REJECTED FAE

SECOND CHANCE SHIFTER ROMANCE

SHERYL NORBUT

Cover Designer: GetCovers.com
Format Designer: Dawn Baca
Gold Deco Curlicue: Roark@Pixaby.com
Chapter Images:
Wolf Head And Stars@Pixy.org
Tribal Wolf@Pixy.org

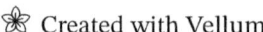 Created with Vellum

CONTENTS

CHAPTER I
PAIGE

Weeds and downed branches bite into my ankles as I sprint through the dense forest that surrounds the Fae Queen's clan compound. Humiliation and despair propel me forward. My steps land in sync with my heartbeat, the sound masking my sobs. Tears stream down my face and my chest burns as my lungs seek air, but all I can focus on is the sting of rejection, again.

It's my own fault. I let myself believe I could be unconditionally loved and accepted. It was naive to believe a Fae prince would want to marry me. Yet, the prince's rejection rips through my soul, tearing my heart to shreds.

As I flee deeper into the damp, endless woods, my thoughts drift back to the Fae queen, my beloved mentor. Since the day I sought her out at the age of eighteen, Queen Sebille has always been there for me, guiding me through the bewildering journey of discovering my powers of telekinesis and healing small wounds. And it was the queen who orchestrated the arranged marriage with the Fae Prince of an opposing clan, hoping to mend the strained relationship between the two clans. I was eager to repay the queen's kindness, quick to agree to the union, believing the marriage was my destiny. I was desperate to prove my worth, to both the beloved queen and to myself. But Prince Beckett, the betrothed Fae prince, snatched that opportunity away in an instant. And all because he discovered I am only half Fae.

An abomination is what Beckett called me when he found out I'm a hybrid. His words were heavy and cruel, and I replay them in my mind over and over until I'm sure I'm about to go mad.

As I continue to run my legs protest, buckling from underneath me, causing me to fall to the ground on my back. I lay there, staring at the millions of stars above me through the canopy of trees. Hopelessness seeps in and I release a loud, gut-wrenching scream into the nothingness around me.

I'm lost in my thoughts when a nearby twig snaps. Bolting upright and jumping to my feet, I look around and even though I can't make much out in the dark, something feels... off. I tense, my senses on high alert. Before I can react, a dark, shadowy cloaked figure lunges at me, dragging me back down to the ground.

A startled scream escapes my lips once again as my head makes impact with the ground. Something unseen has me pinned and I push against it with all my might, but it keeps shoving me back down. My panicked instincts take over as I lift a trembling hand and reach out into the empty space around me hoping something can be 'conjured'. My fingertips call to the invisible energy in the air, summoning it to gather in my palms.

But as the power responds to my call, something unexpected occurs. Instead of a mere manipulation of the air, a spark ignites, and a small spark materializes in my hands. I watch as the flame defies my initial expectations, then continues to grow into a massive fireball.

Flames erupt around my body, somehow siphoning the cloaking field from around my attacker before engulfing him in a raging inferno.

"What the hell?" I whisper to myself as my assailant flops onto the dirt beside me.

He writhes in agony, engulfed by the force of my newfound elemental manipulation, fire and air. The man's white beard singes and the stink of burning keratin wafts around us, a stark reminder of the power I've unleashed.

The fire dies down a bit as I start shaking. I try to focus on keeping the flame lit just enough to keep the attacker at bay.

"I've had a really shit day, old man," I tell him through gritted teeth. "What do you want from me?"

He groans and shakes his head, refusing to speak. I take a step forward and wind my arm back, prepared to strike another blow when his eyes go wide and he shouts, "All right, I'll tell you what you want to know. Just put the fire out."

I draw back the energy and allow the flames to reduce but I'm not about to put the flame out entirely. "That's the best you're going to get."

The man stands on unsteady legs and swipes at his charred shirt.

"What the hell did you come here for?" I demand, my voice shaking almost as much as his knees. "Who sent you?"

He starts to smile, but winces when the blackened skin on his face tightens. "Prince Beckett," he gasps, his voice strained.

I draw my eyebrows together and shake my head. "The Prince! What about him?"

"He sent me after you."

"But why? He's the one who rejected me. If he thinks I'm going to go back to him after..."

"He sent me to exterminate you like the vermin that you are. He believes you to be an abomination." The man hurls the word at me, knocking the wind from my lungs. It hurts no less coming from his mouth than it did from the prince's.

"He wants you destroyed," he continues.

I drop my hands, releasing the magical fire as I take a step back. "What... What have I ever done to him?" I shout, my voice quivering with a mix of rage and disbelief.

He chuckles at my reaction until his laugh morphs into a coughing fit. Once it subsides, he catches his breath and says, "You're a blemish on his kind; a danger to the blood-line, as he put it. Personally, I think the lot of you are mutants, but he pays me well enough to forget he's one of them."

"The queen," I reason with myself out loud, "she wouldn't allow this."

"Prince Beckett doesn't require the permission of a queen from a land which is not his."

"My head is worth a war to him?"

"I'd wager he thinks your head is worth a war with Queen Sebille," he contends.

"That's not true." My stomach twists and sweat peppers my forehead. My energy is waning, giving way to my emotions. He's distracted me, I realize, and I push back at the urge to crumble.

"Perhaps you're right. Fae politics don't concern me, girl."

His callousness fuels me and I drive my foot into the ground. A circle of flames surrounds him again, the sweltering heat blasting back at me. "I never asked for this," I scream. "I never asked to be born this way! Why should my bloodline concern him at all?"

He cowers in the center of the enflamed circle, struggling to speak amidst the smoke. "He fears your power, your potential."

My mind races as I try to piece it all together. Queen Sebille must've used my powers as a selling point when arranging the marriage. Once Prince Beckett called off the marriage, he no longer saw my strength as an asset, but as a threat.

"If he fears my power," I start through gritted teeth, "then he should see what I'm truly capable of."

I take a deep breath, channeling the seething energy within me and a surge of energy courses through me, filling my being with a newfound strength. The circle of flames intensifies, crackling with a ferocious power as the air around me whips in response to my will. His eyes widen in horror as he realizes he has underestimated me.

"No one," I say, my voice dripping with determination, "will destroy me. Not Beckett and certainly not you."

He stumbles back, tripping over his own feet in a desperate attempt to escape the encircling flames. I cut my arms through the air, releasing a burst of wind that knocks him off balance. As he stumbles, I seize the opportunity, conjuring a tornado of flames that engulfs him entirely. The searing heat immerses the surrounding area, casting an eerie glow on the trees with shadows that dance like specters.

My fury begins to ebb, replaced by a sense of justice. I draw back the energy, allowing the flames to subside until only a flickering ember remains. The man collapses to the ground, gasping for air, his clothes smoldering. He releases a blood-curdling scream before he falls silent.

Even as I subdue my assailant, I know the battle is far from over. Beckett's hatred and fear will not be so easily quelled. I must find a way to protect myself from his wrath.

I extinguish the flames and straighten my spine, casting a determined gaze into the depths of the forest. With a heavy sigh, I take a moment to gather my thoughts and regain my composure. The forest around me is filled with an eerie stillness now. I know I can't stay here for long; I must find a safe haven, a place where I can regroup and plan my next move.

The words of the attacker echo in my mind. Prince Beckett believes me to be an abomination, a danger to his precious bloodline. His prejudiced views condemn me based on something I have no control over. But his fear only fuels my determination to prove him wrong.

My attacker lies lifeless; scorched and burned beyond recognition. My breath catches in my throat and I stare at my outstretched hands. The flames I unleashed were powerful, too powerful and I suddenly realize I've taken a life. The weight of that realization settles heavily on my chest.

Around me, the forest is seemingly holding its breath, as if mourning the life lost to my newfound powers. The magnitude of what I have done begins to sink in and I am consumed by regret and sorrow. How could I have let myself be consumed by anger and fear to the point of causing harm?

Tears well up in my eyes, my vision is blurred as I sink to my knees. I reach out, wanting to undo what I've done, to turn back time and make things right. But the forest remains silent, offering no solace or forgiveness.

The guilt envelops me, its suffocating grip squeezing my heart. I cannot let myself become the monster that Prince

Beckett believes me to be. I must learn to control this power, to harness it without letting it consume me. I can't afford to be reckless. My every move must be calculated.

But, where am I to go? I can't go back to Queen Sebille and risk putting her in danger, too.

With a heavy heart, I push myself up from the forest floor, my legs shaky and weak. I take a deep breath, determined to learn from this dark moment and grow stronger. I will carry the weight of this death, but I will also use it as a reminder to temper my anger, to find a better way to channel my power.

I can do this.

I head into the darkness again, knowing I'm too sore and exhausted to go very far this time. As I make my way through the dense forest, guided by the pale moonlight filtering through the thick canopy, I can't help but think of Queen Sebille. She has been a pillar of support in my life since I found her, a guiding light through the darkness. My chest aches from guilt. Not only did I fail to bring about the reconciliation she hoped for, but now, because of me, her clan could be dragged into a conflict over my very existence.

The night wears on and I find myself reaching a clearing bathed in silvery moonlight. It is a tranquil spot, a sanctuary amidst the chaos that surrounds me. I take a moment to breathe in the cool night air, allowing its gentle caress to soothe my battered soul.

In this moment of respite, I make a silent promise to myself and to those who have placed their faith in me. I will not let Prince Beckett's hatred define me. I will rise above his narrow-mindedness and prove that I am deserving of love, acceptance and respect.

With each step forward, I carry the memory of the life lost and the pain it has caused. It will fuel my determination to make a difference, to show the world that even in the face of darkness, there is still a glimmer of light. And I will fight to ensure that my legacy is one of compassion, understanding and forgiveness.

Paige, the hybrid with a heavy heart, will find her way back to the light.

CHAPTER 2
BLAKE

"The forest is quiet tonight," I remark to my beta in our minds as we trek through the dense forest, shifted and on the hunt. We've moved ahead of the pack, searching for our next kill, and so far, we've come up short. "Perhaps we should've stayed close to home."

"*Game is typically much more plentiful out here.*" Jamie freezes in place, and his golden eyes glint off the moonlight as he sniffs at the air around us. "*You smell that, boss?*" he asks.

I take in a long, savoring whiff. Blood mingles with smoke, overpowering the crisp night air that smelled so clean just moments ago. On the edge of it, something soft and feminine lingers, like a mixture of jasmine and the sea. It's a strange collision of smells and I take a step toward it.

"*Yes,*" I reply, my voice barely a whisper. "*It's like nothing I've ever encountered before.*"

Leaves rustle behind me and I turn to find Jamie pacing. Temptation is seeping into my beta's senses. The urge to hunt is eating at him.

"Take it easy," I tell him with a stern edge in my voice, but my words are drowned out by a man's agonizing screams in the distance.

Jamie's brows furrow as he looks at me, his wolf instincts kicking in. *"Do we pursue it, Blake?"*

I consider his words carefully, my mind filled with curiosity and a growing sense of unease. The pack's safety is paramount, but there's something about that scent that tugs at my own instincts, at my soul, beckoning me forward.

"Go," I command, my voice firm. *"Gather the rest of the pack that have come with us in the forest. We need to investigate. But be cautious, Jamie. We don't know what we're dealing with."*

Jamie nods, his golden eyes reflecting understanding. With a swift turn, he disappears into the darkness, his form blending seamlessly with the shadows. As the minutes tick by, I remain rooted to the spot, my senses heightened and my mind racing with possibilities.

The metallic tang of blood grows stronger, intermingled with the acrid scent of smoke. It is a volatile combination that sends a surge of urgency through my veins. I know we cannot afford to rush into this blindly. The safety of my pack depends on some quick, but careful, planning and cautious action.

Soon, the familiar howls and rustling of the pack members

echo through the night. One by one, they gather around me in wolf form, their eyes gleaming with determination and loyalty. I scan their faces, seeing the strength and unity that lies within each member. Together, we are a force to be reckoned with.

Jamie steps forward, his voice low yet commanding. *"Alpha, we are ready to move. The pack is assembled, and we await your orders."*

I quickly shift into my human form and raise my hand, signaling for their attention. My line of sight sweeps over the expectant faces, each one filled with a mix of excitement and readiness. "We have a responsibility to protect our own," I declare, my voice resonating with authority. "We must tread carefully. Our enemy is unknown. We will approach with caution, but strike with the force of a thunderstorm."

The pack members growl in agreement, their pack bond solidifying our purpose and I shift back to join them. My bones crack and contort, reassembling into wolf form. My black coat spreads from my abdomen to my back as I fall on all fours, roaring from the effort it takes.

Once I'm turned, I look at Jamie, our eyes locking in silent communication.

"Jamie, take the lead," I command. *"Lead us to the scent but remember to keep your instincts in check. We cannot afford any unnecessary casualties."*

With a nod, Jamie moves forward, his wolf form darting through the tree line with grace and incredible agility as he tracks the scent. The rest of the pack follows him, their movements deliberate and controlled. I take their flank, weaving back and forth to keep the stragglers in check and protecting our backs. As we move through the darkened forest, our senses heightened and our muscles primed, pride swells through me. Our pack is focused and meticulous, rivaled by no other predator on Earth.

The path ahead could be treacherous, filled with unknown dangers and the ever-present threat of conflict. But none of us are alone. We are a pack bound by loyalty and strength, driven by the unbreakable bond that holds us together.

After running and tracking for just a short time, we see in the distance an eerie glow emanating from a clearing. The crackling of flames and the flickering shadows paint a sinister tableau. I can sense the presence of danger, a malevolence that hangs in the air like a dark cloud. But confusingly, it is accompanied by an unbelievable sweet smell.

Eventually, Jamie slows his pace, indicating that we have reached our destination. We all dip low and stalk onward, hidden within the cover of the trees, observing the scene before us.

"Wait!" I tell them, my voice cuts through the tension like a blade. *"Hold your positions!"*

The pack freezes, their eyes shifting from me to the girl who stands in the glow of fire looking down toward the ground focused on something, her eyes wide with fear and defiance. She doesn't notice us, so I take a step closer just as the girl takes off deeper into the forest.

"Should we go after her, Blake?" Jamie asks, but I shake my head no.

"Not until we understand the situation."

As we cautiously approach, we find a man, bloodied and burnt but alive, lying on the ground. His pained groans fill the air as he struggles to sit up, his eyes widening in terror at the sight of the pack surrounding him.

I step forward and shift back to my human form and I study the pitiful looking man. "What happened here?" I demand, my voice a low growl.

Gasping for breath, he manages to croak out his words. "She, she did this." As he points in the direction in which the girl ran. "That girl, she has power."

"Tell me, what did she do?" Judging by what I saw on the girl's face, she was just as horrified by what she'd done as he was. I wasn't prepared to jump to conclusions yet, based on just a few barely coherent words.

The man grimaces, his features contorted with pain. "Paige, the girl, she summoned, fire, powerful magic, like nothing I've ever seen. She easily struck me down. I didn't stand a chance."

"Was she provoked?

"She's dangerous," the man yells, avoiding the question, before he doubles over to cough uncontrollably.

"Sir," Jamie starts, still in wolf form, *"we should track her*

down." To the injured man it was just a glance between the wolf and the man before him.

"We don't know the full story yet," I contend.

"She could hurt someone else."

"Enough," I command, my voice filled with authority. "We will deal with her later. For now, focus on getting this man medical attention."

Jamie directs a few pack members to the man's side, and after they shift into their human form, they lift him gently and carry him away. "Get him to our healer," he tells them. I watch the group disappear into the night. The remaining pack awaits my next move, their eyes trained on me, seeking guidance. I take a deep breath, grounding myself in the present moment. Whatever the truth is, someone that powerful can't be left unchecked in my woods. Jamie was right when he said the girl could hurt someone and if I let her get away, I'd be responsible. And I can't risk the safety of my whole pack, either.

"Let's regroup," I announce, my voice steady. "Jamie, take some warriors with you and hunt the girl. The rest of us will trail from behind in case we're needed. Find this girl Paige and bring her to me."

The pack nods their understanding, their loyalty unwavering. I shift back to wolf, and we disperse, spreading out in a calculated search pattern, navigating through the dense forest with the stealth and refinement of our wolf forms. Our sense of smell and ability to track are unparalleled. Every sense is attuned to the surroundings, scanning for any sign of this girl's presence.

Minutes turn into an hour as we comb through the undergrowth, following the remnants of her jasmine scent that lingers in the air. Something about her smell stirs my insides, but it's too weak to pinpoint why. Anticipation builds within me as the smell gets stronger.

"*She's close,*" I murmur.

A flicker of movement catches my eye. I motion for the pack to halt, signaling them to remain still and silent; the sound of footsteps, light but hurried, draws closer.

Jamie emerges in human form from the shadows with a beautiful blonde girl in his grasp. "I've got her, boss," he announces and shoves the girl down on her knees.

The girl's breath is ragged, her eyes wide with fear. Blood trickles down her forehead, its path jagged from the movement of her head as she trembles. She glances around and holds her breath as she realizes she's surrounded. Her deep blue eyes lock with mine and a shiver runs down my spine.

Her presence is captivating, her aura drawing me in like a moth to a flame. A jolt of recognition courses through me. It's not just her power that sets her apart; it's something deeper, something that resonates within me.

I inhale deeply, my nostrils filled with her intoxicating scent (the sea and jasmine, intermingling in perfect harmony). A surge of emotion sweeps over me, confirming what my wolf instincts have already realized. I quickly shift into my human form.

"She's, she's my fated mate," I whisper, the realization hitting me like a bolt of lightning.

The pack looks at me, confusion etched on their faces. But I can't ignore the pull that exists between us, the unbreakable bond of fate.

"Stand down," I demand with an involuntary growl aimed at Jamie.

"Blake, I don't think…"

"Release her. Now! This girl is not our enemy." I look around, making sure I am being listened to. *How could my mate be my enemy*, I think to myself.

"She is one of us," I call out to the pack.

The pack exchanges glances, their expressions a blend of surprise and curiosity. I have no doubt they trust my judgment, but this is a test even for their brand of loyalty. Jamie is slow to comply, but he releases his grip and dips his head to me in a submissive bow of apology.

I take a cautious step forward and keep my voice uncharacteristically gentle and low.

"Your name is Paige, right?" I say to her. "There's no need to run anymore. We won't harm you."

Paige climbs to her feet and takes a tentative step back, her expression wary and she asks "How do you know my name? Who are you? What do you want from me?"

"I've been searching for you my entire life" I say softly. "You're safe for now. With me."

Paige crosses her arms in front of her stomach and glances at the trees behind her. For a moment, I'm afraid she'll run again. Her toes point away from me and I ready myself for the chase. I won't let her get away now that I've found her.

"I don't understand," she finally says.

I meet her gaze, holding her captive with my words and the depth of my conviction. "I am Blake, Alpha of the Ocala werewolf pack. I believe you are my fated mate. And your name was given to me by a singed man we found back in the clearing from which you ran."

Her eyes widen, disbelief etched across her face. "Fated mate? What does that even mean?"

I approach her slowly; my steps deliberate, ensuring not to trigger any further alarm or fear. "It means that we are destined to be together, connected by a bond that surpasses time and circumstance. Your scent, the way my soul recognizes you even if I don't, it all confirms the undeniable truth."

Paige takes another step back, her brows furrowing. "I. I don't understand. How can you be so sure?"

I pause, searching for the right words to convey the indescribable. "The way you smell, Paige. It's unlike anything I've ever encountered. The intoxicating blend of the sea and jasmine. It's a fragrance that belongs only to you. It ignites a fire within me."

Her expression softens, a hint of curiosity mingling with her lingering fear. "But, I don't even know you."

"You're right. We are strangers to each other. But fate has a way of bringing souls together, even in the most unlikely of circumstances."

I extend my hand, a gesture of trust and openness. "Paige, please, come with me. Let me protect you, guide you, discover more about you."

Paige hesitates, her gaze flickering between my outstretched hand and my eyes. The turmoil within her is palpable, the wariness battling with the glimmer of hope.

Finally, she takes an uncertain step forward, her hand reaching out to touch mine. As our fingers touch, a surge of warmth and electricity courses through me, another confirmation of our unbreakable connection. I move her palm to rest on my chest so she can feel my heartbeat.

"You feel it, don't you?" I ask. "You feel the pull of fate."

Paige's lips part and she tilts her head to the side as she observes me and I can hear her own heartbeat pounding in her chest. She feels it, I realize, even if she doesn't understand it. The pack watches in silent awe, witnessing the profound moment as our souls reach for each other. They understand the significance of this union, their unwavering support and delight evident in their eyes.

I've finally found her.

CHAPTER 3
PAIGE

My ears ring and my body is still buzzing from the recent purge of energy I used against the hunter. Everything feels like a whirlwind, and I struggle to make sense of the events that have unfolded. The clash with my attacker, the surge of newfound magic so far out of my control and now finding myself in the center of a pack of werewolves whose Alpha says we're fated mates. It's been one hell of a day.

As Blake moves closer to me, his striking green eyes never leaving mine, a strange familiarity washes over me. His scent, a mixture of earth and rosemary, seems to ignite a dormant recognition within me. It's an odd sensation, as Fae are not known for their keen sense of smell. Yet, I can't deny the immediate attraction, to him and to his gorgeous body, which pulses through me in his presence.

At their alpha's request to move to the safe house a few miles away, the other wolves have rushed ahead to clear the way, leaving Blake and me an opportunity to speak in private as we trail behind. I'm not sure where we're headed or even why I'm following him in the first place, but this pull between us. He's right, I do feel it. I just can't make sense of it.

"What, What is going on?" I manage to ask, my voice barely above a whisper and a little unsure. "Why were you chasing me?"

Blake's eyes hold an intensity that both captivates and unnerves me. "We smelled something burning in our territory. We sought out the source and saw you fleeing from a half dead man."

My heart lurches into my throat. "Half dead? You said singed before." I repeat his words and the implication rattles me to my core. "He isn't dead?"

"Thankfully, no." The muscles in his jawline flex. "But he did claim it was you who attacked him, Paige. Would you mind explaining that to me?"

Taking a deep breath, I steady myself and find the strength to share my story. "I, I am being hunted because of my magic."

"Magic?" He stops and grabs my hand. "What are you, Paige? A witch?"

I stiffen at the contact and drop my eyes to the moist leaves at my feet. "I'm Fae. Well, half Fae. I'm still discovering my powers. I swear, I had no idea I was capable of such destruction until today."

"And the man, he was the one hunting you?"

"He was hired to kill me."

Blake's fist clenches at his side and a darkness sweeps over his features. "Who hired him?"

"One of the Princes of an area Fae clan. Prince Beckett. We were arranged to marry, but because I'm only half Fae, he'd rather see me dead."

His face contorts and his whole body tightens. "I should've let him die."

"No, no," I insist. "Really, I'm relieved to hear he survived. I hated the idea of taking a life. But, I'm certain once he's recovered he'll come looking for me again."

Blake's expression softens and I detect a flicker of empathy in his eyes. His midnight black hair rests at his broad shoulders, wisping with the breeze as it catches on the wind. "You are not alone in this anymore Paige. I will protect you as my mate, no matter the cost."

His words hold a weight that resonates deep within me. It's a promise, a vow of unwavering dedication. For a moment, I allow myself to trust in his words, to believe that I may not be alone in this chaotic world that has suddenly unfolded before me.

I'm startled when he takes my hand and presses my fingertips against his lips. "Not that I don't believe you can protect yourself. Clearly, you have the ability, but with my pack I offer you the strength and support you need behind you. If you'll allow me and my pack, we will face this threat together."

His touch sends a shiver down my spine; fear but with a growing sense of comfort flowing within me. I look into his eyes, searching for any signs of deception, but all I find is sincerity, determination, and a caring heart.

"But why?" I can't help but ask. Even if I've just met him, I seem to trust his authenticity. I just don't understand it. "Why would you risk your life and your pack for someone like me? We barely know each other."

Blake's gaze never wavers, his eyes searching mine as if seeking a connection that surpasses mere words. "As I said before, Fate has a way of bringing souls together, Paige," he explains, his voice gentle yet unwavering. "There's a bond between us, one that defies logic and explanation. You are my fated mate."

My heart skips a beat and my mind reels at his revelation again. Fated mate? It's a concept I've heard of, but I never thought would apply to me. Yet, standing here before this powerful Alpha, I can't ignore the pull, the magnetic force that seems to pull us together.

"I still don't understand," I whisper, shaking my head as if I'm trying to wake up from a dream. "How can you be so sure? " I ask again.

Blake takes a step closer, his hand reaching out to gently touch my arm, sending shivers down my spine. "Paige, it's not just your magic or our scent. It's something deeper, something that exists within our souls. I can feel it and I believe you can too."

As his palm rests on my arm, I can sense the thrum of his heartbeat beneath his touch. The connection is undeniable and warmth spreads through me, seeming to cojoin our destinies.

I feel a surge of hope and optimism course through me. Not just from his touch, but from the knowledge that I may no longer be alone on this perilous journey. I have found an ally, a confidant and perhaps something more in this mysterious werewolf.

"But what about your pack? Won't they question your decision to protect someone like me?"

Blake's stance remains steady, his conviction unshaken. "They will understand. Our connection, the pull we feel between us, it extends to my pack as well. They will see that protecting you is not just my choice, but the will of our shared destiny."

"Thank you," I whisper, my voice filled with gratitude and a touch of vulnerability. "I never asked for any of this, but I'm grateful for your offer of protection."

Blake's grip tightens around my hand, his touch grounding me amidst my uncertainty of our surroundings. "As the Alpha of the Ocala pack, it is my duty to ensure the safety of my pack, which includes you now."

Tentatively, I meet his intense gaze, my eyes searching for answers. "What do we do now?"

A hint of a smile graces Blake's lips. "We embrace our destinies, Paige. Together, we will face whatever challenges come our way. I will protect you and by extension, so will my pack."

His words hold a weight that resonates deep within me. It's a promise, a vow of unwavering dedication. For a moment, I allow myself to trust in his words.

We begin walking again until, out of nowhere, fatigue grabs hold and I stumble forward. Exhaustion overwhelms me until my surroundings start to sway. My legs give out beneath me and I almost collapse onto the forest floor before Blake catches me. Darkness edges at the corners of my vision and I feel myself fading into unconsciousness. But before I lose all sense of awareness, Blake's voice breaks through the fog, pleading with me to stay with him.

"I've got you," he adds and I press my weight against him.

In that moment, Blake's human form ripples and shifts, his body transforming into that of a magnificent black wolf. He nuzzles against me gently, his warm fur providing comfort.

"*Climb onto my back,*" I hear him say in my mind. I am amazed to hear his voice in my head. As a wolf he can communicate telepathically? The thought had never occurred to me about how they would communicate in wolf form.

Without the energy to protest, I wrap my arms around his

neck, climb on his back and rest my front along his front shoulders and neck. My heart hammers against my ribcage as the realization sinks in that I'm relying on a werewolf to carry me through the treacherous forest. Blake carries me with ease, his wolf form agile and surefooted, navigating the dense undergrowth effortlessly.

As we make our way deeper into the woods, a distant howl echoes through the night, sending a shiver down my spine. Blake's muscles contract beneath me and he stills, his senses on high alert.

"What's wrong?" I ask, my voice quivering with fear.

"*Hold on to me,*" he urges me, his thoughts echoing in my mind. "*That's not one of my wolves.*"

"Who do you think it is?"

"*We're not in my territory right here, or any other pack's, for that matter. It could be another pack traveling through, same as us, but I don't want to take any chances.*"

I tighten my grip on his fur, bracing myself for whatever danger lies ahead. With a renewed sense of urgency, Blake quickens his pace, his instincts as an Alpha guiding us towards safety while tracking his pack. Leaves crunch beneath his paws and the wind whistles through the trees, carrying both an ominous and beautiful sound.

The howls grow louder, closer and a cold sweat breaks out on my forehead. I can feel the beast closing in on us, its pursuit relentless; adrenaline courses through my veins, temporarily jolting me from my exhaustion. I cling onto

Blake's sturdy frame, my hands gripping his fur, drawing strength from his unwavering determination to protect me.

The sounds of pursuit draw near, footsteps echoing through the darkness. But Blake is undeterred, fueled by an unyielding resolve. He pushes himself harder and faster, his muscles rippling under his sleek coat as he races against time. Every step is calculated, every movement purposeful, as if he's waging a battle against the very forces of nature.

Finally, we break through the edge of the forest, emerging into an open field bathed in the ethereal glow of moonlight. Blake lies down to allow me to climb down off him and I marvel at how massive and strong he really is.

"We lost him. We're safe, for now, we're in my territory now." he assures me, his voice a soothing rumble. *"But we need to keep moving. We can't stay here."*

"I agree." I nod, my breaths coming in ragged gasps as I run my hands along my arms, attempting to warm myself from the biting cold that has replaced the comforting heat of Blake's body and fur. The danger may have momentarily receded, but the threat lingers, urging us to press on.

As Blake resumes his human form, his eyes meet mine and I can't help but feel a sense of awe and trust in this inexplicable bond we share. As much as I would love to take the moment to study it, to bathe in how it feels to have met someone with whom I belong, that will have to wait.

Together, we continue our journey to Blake's safe house, our footsteps leaving faint imprints on the dew-kissed grass.

The night surrounds us, filled with uncertainty and the promise of unseen perils. But as we navigate the treacherous path ahead, I find solace in knowing that I am not alone, that I have found an ally and protector in this Alpha who defies my understanding of the world.

Our steps are guided by Blake's instincts, his tracking abilities, and the light of the stars. The moon shines down on us, casting an otherworldly glow on our path. We walk in comfortable silence and with every passing moment I can feel the connection between us deepening, threading our lives together in ways I never thought possible.

As we traverse the terrain totally unknown to me, the forest gives way again to a desolate moor, its tall grasses swaying in the wind. The landscape feels both eerie and strangely beautiful, a haunting backdrop to our journey. In the distance, I spot the silhouette of a dilapidated stone cottage, its roof sagging under the weight of time. It's a humble sanctuary, a refuge hidden amidst the vast emptiness around us.

As we approach the cottage, a soft light spills from its cracked windows. The scent of burning wood and the air fills with the sound of laughter. A sense of relief washes over me as I realize we are not alone anymore. I look at Blake with a questioning tilt in my neck and he offers a reassuring smile.

"We're not the first to arrive," he says. "Jamie and the rest of the pack are already here. I've been following their trail all night."

My heart quickens as we step through the creaking door. The room is bathed in a warm glow, the fire crackling in the hearth, casting dancing shadows on the worn wooden floor. And there, gathered around the fire, is a group of werewolves in their human form, their faces familiar yet unknown to me.

I recognize Jamie, a fierce and charismatic wolf with striking amber eyes, as he stands up when we arrive. I realize he was the one who captured me and brought me to Blake.. His voice rings out with an unrecognizably cheerful ring, "Blake, Paige... right?, you made it!"

The rest of the pack turns their attention towards us and I take in the intimidating sight. They are a diverse group, each with their own unique presence and aura. Among them, I notice a few familiar faces from the encounter in the woods and it makes my mouth go dry. They would've torn me to pieces if Blake hadn't stepped in.

Blake leads me forward, his grip on my hand tightening as if he can sense my fear. "Everyone, this is Paige," he announces, his voice filled with pride and protectiveness. "She is my fated mate."

Whispers and murmurs fill the room as the pack processes this revelation. Jamie steps forward, his eyes filled with warmth and acceptance. "Welcome, Paige," he says, his voice tinged with genuine kindness. "If Blake declares it, you are now a part of our pack."

The other wolves nod in unison. It's an overwhelming moment, to be embraced by this group of powerful beings. I can't help but feel a sense of belonging, as if I've found a second family. But if my time with Queen Sebille has taught me anything, it's that family is fleeting.

"I hope you don't mind, but Blake relayed most of what you told him enroute," Jamie says. "I wasn't eavesdropping. It's just... well, as the pack's Beta, I need to understand every-thing, you know? You've been through a lot, Paige, in part by my own doing. But you're safe here. We will do everything in our power to keep you protected."

I swallow the lump in my throat, gratitude swelling within me. "Thank you," I say, my voice filled with sincerity. "I never expected to find this kind of support, this kind of caring."

Jamie smiles, his eyes sparkling with wisdom. "Fate works in mysterious ways, my dear. I find it's a lot easier when we don't fight against it. She always wins, anyway."

As the pack surrounds us, a sense of camaraderie settles in the room. I feel their acceptance, their strength and I know that together, we can face any challenges that might lie ahead. Blake squeezes my hand, his touch grounding me in this newfound family.

In this cottage, amidst the flickering fire and the embrace of werewolves, could it be that I have finally found a home? With Blake by my side and the pack behind me, I am ready to face the future that awaits me.

CHAPTER 4
BLAKE

I awaken to the gentle rays of the morning sun, its golden hues casting a warm glow upon the room. Memories of the previous night's events flood my mind and a profound sense of responsibility settles upon my broad shoulders. My gaze lands upon the peacefully slumbering form of Paige beside me, her long wavy blonde hair spread around her head like an angel and protectiveness and admiration both swell within me. She's still covered in blood and dirt, but she's still the most alluring creature I've ever laid eyes on. My fated mate seems to have endured so much already. It's a wonder her spirit is still intact. But I'm here now and with every fiber of my being I swear I will protect her with my life.

With a gentle touch, I brush a stray strand of hair away

from Paige's face, revealing a serene expression that belies the turmoil she endured. "I'm here for you, Paige," I whisper, my voice laced with conviction. "I will support and protect you with everything I have."

Paige stirs, her eyes flutter open and she offers me a grateful smile. "Thank you, Blake," she says. "I'm grateful to have you by my side."

"How are you feeling?"

She stretches her arms above her head and groans. "I'm sore, but I'll survive."

"I'm sorry I didn't get to you sooner. I could've handled the Fae hunter and you wouldn't have had to exert yourself so much."

"Are you kidding me?" Her eyes light up as she sits upright, the blanket crumpling into her lap. "If it wasn't for that maniac, I wouldn't even know I could *do* that fire and air thing."

"You tapped into a power you never knew you had," I say, my voice filled with understanding. "You fought back with such tenacity, and you emerged victorious. I'm proud of you, Paige."

Paige's eyes meet mine, a glimmer of gratitude shining in them. "Thank you, Blake."

The sides of my lips lift into a tender smile as I reach out to caress her cheek. "Believe in yourself, Paige," I say with an unshakeable conviction. "I believe you are may be capable of extraordinary things, and together, we can conquer any challenge that comes our way."

As we sit there, basking in the gentle morning light, a sense of calm washes over us. But the remnants of the previous night's turmoil still linger, reminding us of the dangers that still exist. Paige needs solace and relief, a moment to cleanse herself both physically and emotionally.

"Paige," I begin, "I want to take you somewhere, a place where you can get washed up."

She throws her head back and laughs. "I look that terrible, do I?"

"You could never look terrible. You're stunning and beautiful, even caked in blood and dirt."

"Oh good Lord." Her face turns bright red and she jumps out of bed, pulling out the bottom of her shirt to inspect it. "I still have blood on me! I am so sorry, Blake. I forgot all about it."

I chuckle and shake my head. "I'm a werewolf, Paige. A little blood isn't going to scare me away."

"Okay, well is there a shower I can use?"

"Back at my pack cabin, sure."

She looks around, her forehead crinkled in the most adorable way. "Whose house did we sleep in?"

"It's just one of our safe houses. We have a few strategically placed around and throughout the woods."

"Oh, good, so no breaking and entering, then. How far is

your cabin? Because now that you've pointed it out, I could really use that shower."

I take her hand in mine and trace the creases of her palm, still stained with black soot. "I have a better idea. There's a crystal-clear lake close in the north section of my territory that's said to have healing properties. It's secluded, quiet and guarded by a couple of my pack-mates. No one will disturb us there. You can wash away the past and enjoy the peace and quiet."

A flicker of curiosity dances in her eyes and she nods eagerly. "That sounds perfect," she replies, anticipation lacing her voice. "Lead the way, Blake."

I help Paige to her feet; we make our way outside, back into the same trees that brought us together. The sounds of nature surround us, a symphony of birdsong and rustling leaves. I could never tire of Mother Nature's music. As we make our way through the vibrant forest, the towering trees whisper ancient secrets, their branches swaying in a gentle rhythm.

Shortly, we arrive at the glistening lake, its pristine surface shimmering under the morning sun. Its tranquil surface mirrors the azure sky above, inviting Paige to cleanse herself of the night's turmoil and find solace within the cool, clear waters. Jamie waves at us from the other end and four other wolves from my pack pace the perimeter, keeping a close watch on our surroundings.

"Blake, this place is incredible," Paige remarks with her

mouth agape. "Thank you for bringing me here. It's so unbelievably calm. I need this."

"You deserve every moment of peace and tranquility, Paige," I reply. "And I'll make sure nothing disturbs it. Go for a swim."

Her eyes flit across the lake and she bites her lip. "Are they going to watch, too?"

"Jamie," I call out, catching his attention. "We need some privacy. Keep watch from a distance and be ready to sound the alarm if there's any danger."

My beta's expression turns serious and he offers a curt, obedient nod. "You can count on me, Boss."

I turn to Paige to make sure she's satisfied, but she hesitates for a moment, her eyes searching mine, seeking the reassurance she craves.

"It's all right," I promise her. "I won't let you out of my sight."

With a nod, she locks eyes with me and begins to undress, practically daring me to look down as she draws her shirt up over her head. Heat burns across my cheeks and my throat goes dry. The urge to ravage her is almost impossible to ignore, but I push it down to focus on the task at hand. She slips into the cool, clear water, removing her pants only once her bottom half is submerged.

I watch her intently, the tension slowly dissipating from her body as she immerses herself in the healing embrace of the lake. The sun's rays playfully dance upon her skin, casting a radiant glow, as if nature itself acknowledges her strength and resilience.

As I continue to observe, I catch a glimpse of movement from the corner of my eye; one of my guards, unable to resist his curiosity, peeks at Paige from behind a tree. A surge of possessiveness and jealousy jolts through me, emotions I've never experienced with such intensity before.

Without thinking, I bolt around the lake and pounce on the guard, my instincts taking over. My whole-body barrels into his and he lands hard on his back with a thud. I climb on top of him, driving my fist into his jaw. Spit flies from my lips as I growl, loud and threatening. The message is clear to everyone present: Paige is mine and I will not tolerate anyone invading her privacy or showing an inappropriate interest.

The others gawk and stare, but Jamie is quick to approach. He pulls at my arm just as I'm about to swing down on the wolf again, snapping me out of my rage. "Blake, what's going on?"

"I demanded privacy, did I not?" I released the guard, my gaze locked on Jamie, my voice low and demanding. "No one should be watching Paige while she bathes, no one but me."

"I understand why you feel that way, but Blake, we can't keep an eye on Paige without watching her," he gently points out. "We need to respect her need for solitude while ensuring her safety."

My breaths are heavy, my chest rising and falling as I grapple with my conflicting emotions. I know that Jamie's words hold truth and that unity among the pack is crucial. As much as I'd like to believe that I alone could protect her, I can't watch every inch of the lake's edge on my own.

"You're right, Jamie," I finally concede, looking around at the warriors. Finding Lupe, my sister, I say "We'll find a way to protect Paige without invading her privacy. Lupe, I trust you to move closer and be the one to sound the alarm if there's any danger."

Understanding dawns in Lupe's eyes and she nods in agreement. "I'll protect her with my life, brother," she promises.

As Lupe takes her position, I turn my attention back to Paige, who has sunk down to cover everything below her chin beneath the water. She's noticed the commotion and I can only hope she doesn't think I've overreacted.

"Back to your posts," I bark at the rest of the guards.

With a shared understanding, my wolves adjust their stance, maintaining a vigilant watch over the surroundings while respecting Paige's need for some calm. As promised, my gaze never wavers from Paige. I stand as a silent guardian, ready to shield her from any harm that may come her way.

Paige resurfaces, her soaking blonde hair barely covering her breasts. Uncertainty lingers on her face, and I can sense her question before she even voices it. Moving towards her, I step into the water with my clothes on, the coolness wrapping around my legs.

"I'm sorry for the disturbance," I tell her. "I let my possessiveness get the better of me, but please understand that my intentions were to protect you, not to invade your privacy."

Paige's lips curve into a small smile. "You have a fierce protective streak, Blake."

I reach out to her, taking her hand in mine in a gentle yet firm grip and a wave of warmth passes between us. "I will always protect you, Paige. No matter how fierce I have to get."

"You're going to keep watch from the water? The view is pretty limited."

"The view is spectacular," I counter and waggle my eyebrows.

Suddenly becoming aware of her nipples poking through strands of her hair, Paige covers her chest with her arms. "I hope you enjoyed that show," she teases, splashing water at me with her feet as she swims away.

"I wouldn't even pretend to deny it." I laugh and toss a handful of water in her direction before I follow close.

We swim further into the lake until the water rises above my chest and to her neckline. The sunlight dances on the surface, creating a mesmerizing display of sparkling reflections. Paige closes her eyes, allowing the healing properties of the water to wash over her, cleansing away the remnants of the past and rejuvenating her spirit.

As she stands there, enveloped in the lake's embrace, I can't help but admire her strength and fortitude. The way she carries herself, even in the face of adversity, is nothing short of remarkable. She's a beacon of light and I'm honored to stand beside her.

After some time, Paige opens her eyes, a stillness settling upon her features. She turns to face me, her eyes filled with a renewed determination. "Thank you, Blake," she says, her voice carrying a hint of newfound resolve, "for bringing me here, for offering me your protection and for believing in me."

CHAPTER 5
PAIGE

I follow Blake as he leads me and his pack back to the pack's main cabin in the Ocala Pack compound. My eyes widening in awe at its size and beauty. It's a magnificent structure nestled within the heart of the forest, blending seamlessly with nature. The sturdy logs and intricate craftsmanship speak of a rich history and I can't help but feel a sense of reverence for this place. The other cabins, also made of the same type of logs and workmanship, surrounding the main pack cabin look like individual residence and small local shops.

As we step inside the main cabin, I'm greeted by the warmth of a roaring fire and the comforting scent of wood and earth. The cabin is alive with activity, bustling with pack members going about their daily tasks. Laughter and conversation fill the air, creating an energy that is both welcoming and infectious.

Blake introduces me to his pack-mates, starting with his sister, Lupe, who exudes a friendly and confident aura. Lupe's smile is warm and genuine as she extends a hand in greeting and I instantly feel at ease in her presence. Next is Seth, the gamma, whose calm and composed demeanor commands respect. His piercing gaze holds a depth of wisdom that hints at the trials he has faced as one of the pack leaders.

I'm introduced to the warriors that I haven't met yet, each one displaying strength and loyalty in their own unique way. They share stories and laughter, their brotherhood evident in the way they interact. It's clear that this pack is more than just a group of individuals; they are a family bound by a shared purpose and deep feelings.

After the introductions, Blake takes me on a tour of the cabin. We pass by a spacious common area where pack members gather to relax and unwind, the air filled with the aroma of freshly brewed coffee. The walls are adorned with paintings and symbols, depicting the pack's past, honoring their ancestors.

As we continue our exploration, we reach a small library filled with books and scrolls, a sanctuary for knowledge and reflection. Blake shares with me some stories of their most recent triumphs and hardships that have shaped them into the pack they are today. The walls seem to whisper secrets and wisdom and I can't help but be captivated by the rich tapestry of their heritage.

Finally, we arrive at my own room, a cozy space that reflects the rustic charm of the cabin. The bed is adorned with soft furs and warm blankets, inviting me to rest and find solace. Sunlight filters through the curtains, casting a gentle glow that adds to the room's serene ambiance. It's a place I can truly call my own, a sanctuary where I can gather my thoughts and find respite from the challenges that lie ahead. As I survey my room, my mind wanders to Blake and his room. Is his room close to mine, will we be sharing his room soon? Does Blake even want to share his room with me?

As the evening progresses, the pack gathers outside by a crackling bonfire. The scent of roasted meat fills the air, mingling with the tantalizing aroma of spices and herbs. Pack members take turns cooking the day's kill, their movements synchronized and efficient. The flames dance and flicker, casting a warm glow that illuminates the faces of those gathered around.

I take a deep breath, inhaling the crisp night air as the crackling bonfire casts a warm glow upon the faces around me. The immediate amity and acceptance I feel from Blake's pack fill me with a sense of fitting in like I've never experienced before. It's as if I've found my home amidst this wild and untamed wilderness.

A gentle breeze rustles through the trees, carrying with it the scent of the forest and the distant howls of unseen creatures. The pack members, gathered in a circle around the fire, share more stories and laughter, their voices blending into a harmonious symphony of belonging.

Blake's hand finds mine and a surge of electricity once again courses through me. It's as if a tether has been formed between us, an unbreakable bond that transcends the physical realm. The attraction between us is undeniable, a magnetic pull that defies reason.

Amidst the lively atmosphere, Blake leans over with a playful sparkle in his eyes. "Paige, would you like to dance?" he asks, extending his hand.

A smile tugs at the corners of my lips. "There's no music."

"So we make our own."

I shrug and move with him to stand. As we settle near the fire, I press my body against his and every inch of me comes alive. We sway and move with the sounds around us, finding a rhythm between us that only we can hear. It's as if the world around us fades into the background, leaving only the two of us in this moment of connection. The space between us seems to crackle with anticipation, the air charged with an undeniable chemistry.

Unable to resist the magnetic pull, I lean into him. Heat radiates between us, intensifying the attraction that is so palpable in this shared dance. It's a dance of souls, a convergence of two beings drawn together by a force beyond comprehension.

I'm lost in the whirlwind of emotions. I find myself

allowing my fingers to explore the line of his jaw and brushing thru his beard. His white shirt is buttoned just below the collarbone and his sleeves are rolled up just shy to his elbow. His forearm ripples as he spins me, dipping me down until my hair dances in the dirt. My heartbeat races when our hips collide, moving in unison and grinding together. The burning pull between us is undeniable and I'm consumed by a desire to explore this uncharted territory.

I bite my lip as I observe his dark features and before I can pull it back, I hear my own voice say, "You look the part."

Blake's eyes sparkle with intrigue as he tilts his head, a hint of a smile playing at the corners of his lips. "What do you mean?"

"I mean, you have that alpha presence, that commanding aura. Rugged and terrifying, but still so sexy it makes girls like me forget just how dangerous you are." My face tingles as the blood rushes to my feet. "I can't believe I said that out loud."

A low chuckle rumbles from deep within Blake's chest and he reaches up to brush a stray strand of hair behind my ear. "Paige, you have no idea how much your words affect me," he says, his voice husky, "I can't help but be drawn to every part of you."

I giggle to myself and Blake tilts back, tucking a finger under my chin to lift my face to look at him. "What is it?"

"This is going to sound ridiculous." I say.

"Try me."

"I feel like I know you," I confess. "But, that's impossible, right?"

"You do know me," he assures me.

I lean closer to Blake, my voice barely above a whisper. "I don't understand what's happening, Blake. This connection, this pull between us, it's so strong. I've never felt anything like it before."

He gazes into my eyes, his own filled with a mixture of affection and understanding. "Paige, what we're experiencing is rare and extraordinary. As I've said, we're fated mates. It means we were destined to find each other, to be together. Our souls are intertwined across time and space."

Skepticism and curiosity bubble within me. Yet, as I search his eyes, I can sense the truth resonating deep within my core. There's an unspoken knowing, a connection that defies everything I've ever known but feels undeniably real.

"You mean to say that we were meant to find each other?" I ask, my voice tinged with wonder.

Blake nods, a gentle smile gracing his lips. "Yes, Paige. We were destined to meet, to share this profound bond. It's as if we've known each other for lifetimes."

As if drawn by an invisible force I lean in, closing what little distance there is between us. The warmth of his touch seeps into my skin, sending shivers down my spine. There's a fire in his eyes, a hunger that mirrors my own desires. In that moment, the space between us seems to disappear and the air

crackles with an intensity that is both exhilarating and intoxicating.

"I'm glad I'm not the only one feeling this," I reply, my
voice barely above a whisper. "Being around you, it's like
being under a spell. I can't help but lose myself."

Before another moment can pass, before the doubt can
creep in, our lips finally meet in a passionate and fiery kiss.
Our tongues explore. Our groans are heard. It's a collision of
desires and emotions, a union that transcends words. In that
simple yet profound act, the world seems to tilt on its axis.
Time stands still as the kiss deepens, conveying emotions that
words fail to capture.

In that moment, my heart swells with a sudden rush of
devotion not just for Blake but for his entire pack. I can feel
the string that binds them together, an unbreakable thread of
loyalty and love. Their acceptance of me, their willingness to
open their hearts and embrace me as one of their own, fills
me with a profound sense of gratitude.

As our lips part, I find myself enveloped in the loving
gazes of the pack members around us. Their smiles hold a
mixture of approval and joy, a silent affirmation of our
connection. In their eyes, I see a reflection of the deep love
and commitment that runs through this pack and I know that
I'm now a part of something greater than myself.

"All right," I shout at them. "The peep show is over, fellas."

CHAPTER 6
BLAKE

"Wolves, line up," I bark at my warriors as they assemble in front of me in straight lines, prepared to train. I scan their faces, taking a tally of who has answered the call. "Jamie, where's my sister?"

Jamie steps forward. "Lupe took the pups into town. She left at dawn, she should be back within the hour."

"Very good." I crouch down and draw up my fists as Jamie steps back into position. "Follow my lead."

Our bodies move in sync as we focus on attack formations and direct contact. We move with precision and agility, honing our skills in both human and werewolf forms. Each wolf pushes themselves to the limits, determined to become stronger, faster and more formidable.

We focus on footwork, an essential skill no matter what

form we are in. We practice evasive maneuvers, swift changes in direction and rapid reactions. The ground beneath us trembles as we move, leaving a trail of dust and fallen leaves in our wake.

Sweat beads on my brow from the unexpected beating heat as we execute complex maneuvers, seamlessly transitioning between offensive and defensive techniques. The sound of heavy breathing and the clashing of teeth and claws echo through the training grounds. The atmosphere is charged with anticipation, every movement deliberate and purposeful.

I step to the side to observe my pack closely, their muscles rippling with power, their eyes gleaming with determination. Each member embodies the spirit of a warrior, fully committed to the pursuit of excellence. Their commitment to training is not just about physical strength; it's about forging an unbreakable team, fostering trust and honing their instincts.

We move on to practice strategic formations, moving as one cohesive unit. The pack warriors shift and flow, their movements synchronized to create a fiercesome force. I guide them through various scenarios, simulating real-life combat situations, ensuring that they are prepared for any eventuality.

Paige watches us from the deck of the cabin while working on taming her own powers. She stretches out her arms and waves her hands, trying to recreate the elemental manipulation she let loose on the Fae hunter. Eventually, frustration gets the better of her and she drops her arms and flops onto a porch swing hanging near the front door. The swing creaks under her weight as she sits down, disappointment dragging her shoulders to slump. Sensing her struggle, I make my way toward her, leaving the pack to continue their drills under Jamie's watchful eye.

I approach Paige, wiping the sweat from my brow with the back of my hand, my muscles pulsating with exertion. I sit beside her on the swing, our bodies slightly touching and take a moment to catch my breath.

"You're doing great, Paige," I tell her. "Harnessing and controlling your powers take time and practice. Remember, it's not about forcing it, but about finding that balance within you to create the power when you need or want it."

Paige sighs and looks at me, her eyes filled with frustration and a hint of self-doubt. "I know, Blake, but it's frustrating. It's like the fire and air elements only respond when I'm in grave danger or very angry. I want to be able to use them at will, without having to be pushed to the edge."

"I don't care to ever see you pushed to the edge again, even if it's to test your powers."

"Your pack is lucky. They've got you to teach them. I had the queen, and she did her best to help me, but I don't think even she would know how to handle this type of magic. I've never heard of this kind of elemental manipulation."

"I have complete faith in your abilities, Paige. With time

and practice, you'll gain the control you seek. Just remember, it's not just about the power itself, but also the intention behind it."

She leans into my touch and rests her head on my shoulder. "Thank you, Blake. Your belief in me means the world."

I smile, squeezing her shoulder gently. "You don't have to thank me, Paige. We're in this together."

"Blake!" Lupe suddenly bursts onto the training grounds, hair and dirt caked onto her face. Pups trail behind her in their shifted form, whimpering and crying. "Something emerged from the woods," she exclaims, her voice laced with panic. "It snatched one of the pups and disappeared!"

The atmosphere shifts instantly, the focus of the training session shattered by the urgent call to action. Without hesitation, my pack swiftly shifts into our wolf forms, our bodies transforming into sleek and powerful creatures. The seamless metamorphosis binds us together as a terrifying unit, fueled by a primal instinct to protect our own. Every muscle quivers with readiness, every nerve pulsates with anticipation. We become a unified force, ready to track down the attacker and retrieve the kidnapped pup.

As one, the pack warriors, surrounding me, surge forward into the forest, our paws pounding the earth with remarkable speed. The forest becomes a blur of green as we slice through the dense foliage, leaving behind a trail of rustling leaves and the echo of our determined howls. The scent of the assailant hangs in the air, its acrid presence a bitter reminder of the danger lurking within our sacred territory. The smell is known, it's the hunter that attacked Paige, and that we helped heal.

The chase becomes a thrilling dance of agility and cunning as we navigate the labyrinthine paths of the woods. Our senses heighten, every flicker of movement and scent woven into the fabric of our instincts. We are hunters, honed by centuries of survival, propelled by an unyielding resolve. Each stride, each calculated turn, brings us closer to the truth concealed within the shadows. Our paws pound against the ground, leaves and branches rustling beneath our weight.

As we track the hunter and cub, their scent takes us on many twists and turns, like an ethereal serpent leading us deeper into the heart of the mystery. It circles around the pack compound, teasing us with its proximity before plunging back into the woods. We follow the winding trail, our wolf instincts guiding us closer to the truth.

We keep tracking the targets around the cabin, then suddenly, their scent leads straight back to the main pack cabin. As we close in on the cabin, dread pools in the pit of my stomach. The realization hits me like a physical blow; the kidnapping of the pup was nothing more than a diversion, a calculated maneuver to draw us away from the intruder's true target.

Panic sets in as we arrive at the cabin and I see Paige standing on the porch, a small ball of fur in one arm struggling to jump down. In her other hand, a dying fireball flickers, struggling to maintain its flame. She glares at something invisible in the distance, searching for something or someone in the field.

"*Lupe! Get the pups inside.*" I command, my tone sharp and rough with authority. "*The rest of you, secure the perimeter. Protect Paige and the pups at all costs.*"

Paige's eyes widen with alarm as she realizes the imminent peril. She startles at my voice and releases the remnants of magic still simmering in her palm to clutch the pup against her chest, soothing him until Lupe collects him and takes him inside with the others.

My wolves form a protective circle around the cabin, our muscles tense, ready to face whatever danger awaits. Paige steps beside me in front of the porch, stroking the top of my head in a show of solidarity.

"It was him," she tells me. "The Fae hunter. He told me he used the pup to draw you away, so he could come after me."

I curl my claws into the dirt, anger surging through my veins at the audacity of the Fae hunter. My eyes scan the surroundings, searching for any sign of the intruder. "*He won't get away with this,*" I growl.

"We can't let him harm anyone else because of me."

"*This isn't your fault, Paige. Don't you dare blame yourself.*"

"Regardless of whose fault it is, we need to stop him."

I nod, my gaze fixed on the field. "*We will. But we must be cautious. He's cunning and dangerous.*"

Paige's eyes meet mine and her hand brushes against my

fur in a gesture of reassurance. "I don't care how powerful he is. He came after a pup, Blake. That can't stand."

A chorus of agreement ripples through the pack. They heard Paige's words to me and they resonate with my pack, with a deep sense of righteousness, fueling the flames of determination within us all. I take solace in the unwavering support of my pack, knowing that we stand united in our resolve to protect the innocent and ensure that justice is served.

"He won't escape justice," I declare. *"We'll find him and we'll make sure he never threatens us again."*

With renewed purpose, we fortify our positions around the cabin, each member of the pack ready to defend against any potential threat. Anticipation thickens the air around us as we scan the surroundings for the slightest sign of the hunter's return.

"Jamie, take six warriors and continue to search the surrounding area for the hunter." I order. *"The rest of you warriors, stay in your positions around our compound and protect the cubs and Paige."*

Paige's hand remains on my fur, a constant source of comfort and strength. I lean into her touch, drawing reassurance from our connection. Together, we are an unyielding force, a beacon of protection against the darkness that seeks to harm our pack.

"We are stronger together, Paige. And we will prevail."

As darkness settles over the land, we remain vigilant, our

senses on high alert. The scent of the Fae hunter lingers in the air, a dark presence that taints the serenity of the forest.

Hours pass, the night deepening and still, the hunter eludes us. He has probably left our territory by now. But our determination never wavers. We search every shadow, follow every scent, our pursuit unwavering. The safety of our pack and the protection of our realm drive us forward.

CHAPTER 7
PAIGE

The next morning, grateful smiles and pats on the back follow me everywhere I go on Blake's property as his pack-mates express their appreciation for me 'saving' their cub. Their words of praise echo in my ears, but deep down, I feel a sense of exhaustion creeping in.

I close myself in the pack house, away from the excessive adoration for a moment. Finally alone, I allow myself to stretch my neck and crumple to the ground against the wall. My body aches with weariness. Trying to control the fire element again, warding off the hunter, staying vigilant all night searching for the creep, has drained every ounce of my energy.

"You look like shit."

I jump at Lupe's voice. "Sorry. I didn't realize anyone was in here. I can go back outside if..."

"Don't be ridiculous. Come on upstairs. I caught a glimpse of you limping around outside and drew you a bath."

"Lupe, you're my savior."

Lupe grins, her eyes twinkling with warmth. "Consider it payback for saving our pup, Paige. Now, come on, let's get you cleaned up."

As I follow Lupe up the stairs, each step feels like a victory and a burden all at once. The cabin's upper floor is cozy and inviting, filled with the familiar scents of the pack. Blake's smell stands out and I hold onto it for strength.

As we enter the bathroom, I'm greeted by the sight of a steaming bath filled with fragrant herbs and petals. The room is softly lit, casting a warm glow that soothes my tired eyes. Lupe gestures for me to step in, her eyes filled with understanding.

"Go on, Paige," she encourages, her voice gentle. "Soak away the weariness and let the warmth of the waters work their magic."

I strip off my dirt-streaked clothes, revealing bruises and scrapes that bear witness to my battle with the Fae hunter while trying to hold a scared cub in one of my arms. The soothing water embraces me as I sink into its depths, the tension in my muscles slowly easing away.

Lupe sits on the edge of the tub, a comforting presence by my side. She picks up a washcloth and washes the back of my neck, the heat seeping into my muscles and coaxing them to relax.

"You did well, Paige. We couldn't have asked for a better mate for our alpha."

Her words bring a flicker of pride amidst the weariness. I sink deeper into the water, closing my eyes and allowing the soothing properties of the bath to wash over me. The scent of lavender and chamomile fills the air, easing my senses.

"You were amazing too, Lupe," I respond, my voice soft. "Your speed and agility were invaluable. Who knows what that monster would've done to that pup if you hadn't gotten to the rest of the pack so fast."

Lupe chuckles. "That's what packmates are for, Paige. We support each other through thick and thin. And trust me, there's a lot of thick."

Silence envelops us for a moment, the only sound is the soft lapping of water against the sides of the tub. The sound is hypnotic and distracting and finally the weight of the night's events begins to lift.

"I'm glad to see you're taking a moment to recover." I bolt up in the tub at the sound of Blake's voice. A playful grin spreads across his face as he steps further into the room. "I didn't mean to startle you."

I purse my lips together and blow out a steady stream of air. "Sorry, I'm still a little jumpy. You've got to remember I don't have your wolf ears, Blake."

Lupe places a comforting hand on my shoulder before looking at her brother, who gestures his head toward the door. "Thanks for taking care of her, Lupe."

"Of course." Lupe stands and hugs Blake before turning back to me to say, "Get some rest, Paige."

The door closes behind her, leaving us alone.

As Blake approaches, my heart skips a beat. He kneels next to me, wrapping a hand around my neck to bring my forehead to his lips. I'm naked and vulnerable and my fatigue is making it difficult to keep up the facade of strength. But his touch, his presence, has a way of grounding me. I melt into his arms, finding solace in his embrace.

I take a deep breath, my voice barely a whisper as I convey the hunter's ominous words. "He swore he'd be back with an army," I confess. The worry clenches at my heart, threatening to consume me.

Blake's voice, soothing and steady, reaches my ears. "Don't worry about it right now," he reassures me, his words a lifeline amidst the storm. "I will protect you and my pack. We will face whatever comes together."

As the water touches gently against my skin, Blake takes charge His hands tenderly moving over my body. He massages away my any tension I still have, washing away not only the physical fatigue but also the burdens weighing on my mind. I surrender to the sensations, my desires quickly surfacing, and my need for Blake blooming hot.

Blake slips a finger under my chin and tilts my face to look at him. Longing burns between us. My breath is caught in my throat when I place my hands on either side of his cheeks and pull him closer. Our lips meet and a wave of warmth and craving washes over us. The kiss is gentle yet filled with a fervent yearning, a reaffirmation of the bond we share.

Time seems to stand still as we lose ourselves in each other, the worries and exhaustion of the outside world fading into the background. In this moment, it is just the two of us, finding comfort and strength in each other's embrace.

Lifting me carefully from the bath, Blake carries me to the bed, his touch igniting a fire within me. Water drips from my body, soaking the sheet beneath me, but I'm too focused on the look of primal need on Blake's face to care. The boundaries between us blur and we give in to the overwhelming passion that engulfs us.

He straddles my naked frame reclaiming my mouth with his. I arch my back, pressing my body against his, but it isn't enough. I pull away just long enough to tear Blake's shirt over his head, craving his skin against mine. His hand cups my breast, the delicate skin of my nipples searing under his hot breath as he takes one in his mouth, teasing my bud with his tongue. He works small circles around the pink flesh before moving on to the next.

My lips part as I moan through ragged breaths. I fumble with the buckle of his pants, too distracted by the pleasure coursing through every inch of my body to concentrate on undoing it. Blake chuckles at my impatience as his focus shifts and he trails his lips down my abdomen, taking his manhood out of reach. My body erupts into ecstasy as he descends to explore my folds. Licking and sucking my nub until I whimper and groan, begging him to enter me. Seeming satisfied with my pleas, Blake nibbles at my inner thigh before removing his pants and climbing on top of me.

As he enters me, gently at first and then with more aggressive thrusts, his head falls back and he releases a low, animalistic growl, his muscles undulating with each drive. My body quivers under him and my hands roam across his chest, pinching each of his nipples, before I reach up and pull him closer, needing to feel every inch of him against me.

As our bodies move in harmony, a crescendo of pleasure envelops both of us. In the throes of our coupling, Blake's teeth graze the delicate skin between my neck and shoulder and, after asking for my permission, bites down to leave his mark, leaving an indelible mating sign; a show of love and possession. It is a symbol of our union, forever binding us together.

In the aftermath of our passion, a sense of exhilaration washes over us. Some of our powers, once separate, are now shared and complement each other. We have become more than just two individuals, we are one, sharing our strengths and vulnerabilities.

An enhanced ability emerges with the pack, as if a telepathic thread already sewn, now connects our minds and our emotions more deeply and I can now feel the connection to all pack members. Words need not be spoken. Blake and my thoughts effortlessly dance between us. It is a profound connection, a testament to our bond and I revel in the knowledge that we are now mates, forever entwined in this extraordinary journey.

As we lay together, bodies wrapped around each other, I find solace in Blake's arms. The world may be filled with uncertainties and threats, but in this moment, in his embrace, I feel safe. And with our shared powers and newfound telepathy, we can face the challenges that lie ahead, united in love and unwavering determination.

CHAPTER 8
BLAKE

"You look rested," my beta, Jamie, says with a knowing smile.

He is not wrong. A sense of calm has replaced my busy mind. My body is still reeling from my time spent with Paige and as hard as I've tried, I can't wipe this stupid grin from my face. "I've had a good morning," I admit. "But we're still on high alert."

"Of course. Where's Paige?"

I point at the deck, where Paige is curled up on the swing reading. "After everything, she's been through recently, I won't let her out of my sight again."

"I don't blame you. That was a close call. Thank God she was there to save the pup, though."

I nod, acknowledging the compliment to my mate. "Can you gather the pack? We have matters to discuss."

"You got it, boss."

Jamie shifts and takes off and one by one, my wolves assemble in front of me. Their presence brings a sense of comfort and pride, reminding me that we stand together in the face of danger. As their alpha, it is my duty to ensure their safety and protect my fated mate.

After the pack gathers before me, I clear my throat, commanding their attention.

"Pack-mates," I begin, my voice carrying the weight of authority. "Last night, we faced a threat in the form of the Fae hunter. His attempt to harm Paige and the pup will not go unanswered. We must remain vigilant and prepared for his return, for he has vowed to come back with an army."

Murmurs ripple through the crowd in front of me. Lupe, seeming to sense the growing unease, steps forward, her voice carrying across the gathering. "Paige could've run when the hunter arrived, but she didn't. She faced the hunter on her own and saved the life of that pup."

At her words, I straighten my spine, projecting my admiration and support for Paige onto the crowd.

"She has proven her loyalty and her commitment to our pack," Lupe adds. "And I stand with her."

I half expect protests or suggestions from some of the pack members, to send Paige away to rid ourselves of the danger. But to my surprise, they simply look on, seeking more information and answers.

At that moment, overcome by my own devotion to Paige, I

hold out my hand in her direction. "Paige, come, I need to show them."

She focuses on me, chewing on her bottom lip as she takes in the stares from the pack. She takes slow, hesitant steps, but when she reaches my side, she stands tall, a testament to our united front. The pack's eyes shift to her, their expressions filled with respect and gratitude.

"By now, you all know Paige is my fated mate. But she is also an integral part of our pack." I brush her hair to the side and draw their attention to the mark I have left on her, a symbol of our bond and the commitment we share. "She is not just my partner, but she is now your Luna, interlinked with the very fabric of our pack."

The cheers that erupt from the pack are deafening, echoing through the air. They express their acceptance loudly, their voices carrying a sense of knowing this truth. With Paige as our Luna, the harmony of the pack is stronger than ever.

As the cheers subside, I feel an overwhelming sense of gratitude. I am blessed with a pack that stands by me, a mate who complements me in every way and a love that transcends the ordinary. We are not just a pack; we are a family, bound together by loyalty and unwavering support.

Paige lifts her chin, flexing her jaw as she fights against her own nerves. "I may not have the same abilities or instincts as a werewolf, but I pledge myself to this pack. I am committed to protecting our home, as I consider this my home now too, and the lives within it," she asserts, her voice carrying a quiet strength.

I lace my fingers with Paige's, symbolizing our connection and solidarity. "This hunter seeks to exterminate your alpha's mate. We will face the Fae Hunter together, as one family. Our combined strengths will be our greatest defense."

The pack responds with a unified howl, their voices blending in a song of the wolf. It is a declaration of their support for both Paige and our collective cause. Their eyes, filled with fierce determination, meet mine and Paige's, confirming their commitment to protecting their newfound pack-mate.

Paige's grip on my hand tightens and a smile tug at the corners of her lips.

"We have strengthened our defenses," I start again once the noise has died down, "but we cannot let complacency creep in." My gaze sweeps across the attentive faces before me. "I want patrols doubled, especially around the perimeter of our territory. We must remain alert for any signs of the Fae hunter or his allies."

"Paige played a pivotal role in thwarting the Fae hunter's plans," I announce, pride lacing my words. "Her bravery and quick thinking saved the pup and brought us closer to unraveling the evil surrounding this threat." Paige stands tall, but her cheeks turn pink with embarrassment.

"But we cannot rely on one individual," I emphasize, my tone firm. "This is a battle we face as a pack. Each one of you holds a crucial role in our defense. We will train harder, sharpen our skills and be ready for whatever 'army' comes our way."

The pack responds with resounding growls of agreement, their determination echoing through the clearing. They understand the importance of each member drawing strength from one another.

"Remember," I conclude, my voice tinged with conviction, "we are stronger together. We will not be intimidated by the Fae hunter's threats. We will protect our territory, our loved ones and each other. Our bond as a pack is unbreakable."

Paige remains by my side, her presence a calming influence and an inspiration. In her, I find a love and connection that surpasses all boundaries.

With a final glance exchanged between us, we turn our attention to the tasks at hand. The pack disperses, each member resuming their assigned positions, ready to defend our territory and prepare for the battle that looms on the horizon.

In the days that follow, our pack rallies around Paige, ensuring her safety and providing protection. The guards I assigned are diligent in their duties, patrolling the territory with heightened vigilance and training ferociously. We have become a fortress, a solid front against the threats that seek to harm us.

Paige's presence among us brings a renewed sense of purpose and determination. Her gentle, sassy and challenging soul inspires us all, reminding us of what we fight for. She embraces her role as Luna within the pack with grace and courage, becoming an integral part of our community.

In the evenings, after the daily preparations for a battle have been made and the pack settles down, I find myself seeking refuge in Paige's embrace. As our bodies make love and our thoughts and emotions are shared, our souls are moving even closer.

Together, Paige and I will navigate the treacherous path that lies ahead. We are prepared to face the hunter and his promised army, knowing that our pack stands firmly by our side.

CHAPTER 9
PAIGE

Blake and I find a quiet spot amidst the flurry of the pack's activities and preparations. It's a type of respite, a chance for me to delve deeper into my powers with Blake's guidance, a step towards controlling and mastering my elemental abilities without the aid of Queen Sebille.

Blake's brows are stitched together, his concentration unshakeable. He presses his palms against the back of my hands, guiding their movements and I allow him to lead.

"Focus, Paige," he gently reminds me. "Find the stillness within you and let it guide your connection with the elements."

I hang onto his every word, eager to absorb his knowledge. He may not possess the same magic I do, but his ability to not only master his shifting and command the entire pack cannot be understated. His experience is invaluable and I respect it. However, the touch of his hand against mine sends electric currents through my body every single time, making it a challenge to fully concentrate on the task at hand.

"Feel the static in the air," he tells me and I reach for the sensation with my fingertips. "The magic is already there. You just need to harness it. Bend the energy to your will. Demand its submission."

I close my eyes, taking deep breaths to steady my racing heart. As Blake's instructions echo in my mind, I visualize the air surrounding me. I summon it, feeling its invisible embrace. Slowly, I open my eyes and there it is; the gentle sway of leaves. A small accomplishment of using air, but one I let seep into my being as proof I can do this.

Blake's eyes light up with pride as he witnesses my progress. His grip on my hands tightens slightly, his touch both grounding and disturbing. "Well done, Paige," he murmurs, his voice filled with admiration. "You have a natural affinity for this. With time and practice, you'll become even more powerful."

A rush of excitement courses through me, fueling my determination to delve deeper into my elemental abilities. The gentle sway of the leaves becomes a playful dance, responding to the subtle shifts in my energy. The air responds to my command, a harmonious connection forming between us.

Blake releases his hold on my hands, allowing me to explore this newfound connection on my own. I extend my palms upward, and with focused intent, I channel my energy into the air around me. The breeze picks up, lifting strands of my hair and caressing my skin.

As I'm reveling in the exhilaration of my progress, a sense of unease washes over me. The air around me becomes charged with an unfamiliar energy, tinged with unsettling darkness. Instinctively, I reach out to Blake, seeking his steady presence.

He senses my apprehension and wraps an arm around me, providing a sense of comfort and protection. "What is it, Paige?"

"I, I sense something. Something dark and foreboding," I whisper, my voice barely audible. "It's as if the very fabric of the air is tainted."

Blake's jaw flexes as he scans our surroundings, pulling me tighter against him. "What is it?"

"The hunter. He's close."

The bustling energy of the pack continues, unaware of the underlying danger I perceive. "Stay close to me, Paige," Blake commands, his alpha authority coming to the forefront.

His words embolden me to face the next challenge. "I will," I promise him, "but I have to keep going if we're going to beat this."

I turn my attention to the fire element. I concentrate my energy, envisioning flames flickering in my palms. Drawing upon the core of my being, I allow the heat to surge within me. Suddenly, my hands are ablaze with vibrant flames, dancing with life.

"There it is! Blake, I did it!"

I'm quick to extinguish the flame as Blake turns to me, lifts me at the waist and spins me around. I wrap my arms around his neck and squeeze my eyes shut, relishing the feeling of the world spinning around me.

"I knew you'd get it," he tells me before pressing his lips against mine.

After our training session, we return to the pack. There is still danger in the air. The whole pack can feel it now.

I lift my chin, pride swelling in my chest. The impending darkness and the dread that accompanies it begins to lift. Whether it's because the hunter has left the area or because of my increased confidence, I can't be sure, but either way, my stomach growls, the ache filling the void.

"We should eat," Blake says.

I shake my head and plant my feet again. "Just one more round." Blake agrees and I actually am able to do several more rounds, controlling my call to the elements of air and fire even more practiced.

As the sun begins to set, casting a warm golden glow around us, Blake and I decide to savor the moment. We want to eat by ourselves. So we build a picnic basket full of nourishing treats and settle down on a cozy blanket just a little ways away from the main cabin in the forest. As we indulge in the simple pleasure of food, Blake's eyes study me, curious and questioning. We know this break is nothing more than an interlude before the storm, but we embrace this moment we can share.

"Stop looking at me like that," I tease, throwing a grape at him.

"I can't help it. You are just so beautiful."

"You look like you want to ask me something, Blake. Go ahead."

"It is just, your parents. I've never heard you speak of them. You talk about the queen sometimes, but even that topic seems guarded."

His words steal the air from my lungs. I sit back on my heels and swallow against the sudden dryness in my throat.

"I'm sorry." He reaches for me, but I pull away, afraid if I allow him to hold me, I'll clam up. "You don't have to…"

"It's okay," I assure him, "You deserve to know and I do need to talk about it eventually."

Blake rests an elbow on the ground, shifting his body weight into it. "I'm listening."

It takes all the bravery I can summon and when I finally open my mouth to speak, my voice is shaky and high-pitched. "My mother passed away when I was very young. After that, everything changed between my father and me. We were close when she was alive, but it was like my existence reminded him of her too much and he could not cope. I did not understand it was because he knew I was half-Fae and he had no idea how to explain any of it to me."

"You didn't know?"

"I had no idea. Until I was in high school and out of nowhere, I started making things disappear and blowing things up when I was in a bad mood. And I couldn't talk to my dad about it. I was too afraid of what he would say."

"That must've been terrifying for you to go through all alone." Blake says.

"You have no idea." I snort and shake my head. "Then one day, when I was eighteen, I was in the attic going through some of my mother's things and I found a spell book. It had an inscription from Queen Sebille and somehow, I knew if anyone could help me it was her. So I ran away to find her."

"I cannot believe you found her without any help. That's incredible, Paige."

"It was a lonely path," I admit, my voice tinged with a touch of sadness. "But she became my guide, teaching me the basics of being Fae and unveiling the powers of healing and telekinesis. However, there were still gaps in my knowledge that I had to navigate on my own, as you can see."

Blake's hand finds mine, offering comfort and reassurance. "You've shown immense courage, Paige, seeking out the queen, embracing your heritage. It takes guts to face the unknown."

I smile, grateful for his understanding. "When the queen told me tensions were high with a neighboring clan and that my marrying their prince could help, I was quick to jump in headfirst. I thought it was my destiny; my chance to repay her for everything." I drop my eyes to the blanket beneath me and pick at its fabric. "But he didn't want me."

Blake nuzzles his lips against the soft spot behind my ear. "He's a fool," he whispers before pulling away and brushing his lips against my knuckles. "I, for one, will be forever grateful for his poor judgment."

"But there's still so much I don't know. When I fled from Prince Beckett, I carried so many unanswered questions with me. For example, does the queen know he sent the Fae hunter after me? I just cannot imagine her being okay with it, but maybe... maybe I don't know her as well as I thought I did."

Blake's gaze intensifies, his voice filled with determination. "You're not alone in this anymore, Paige. You have me and the entire pack by your side. We won't let anyone harm you."

His words touch my heart and I lean closer to him. "Thank you, Blake. I can't express how much it means to me to have you all here, supporting me."

Blake's lips meet mine in a tender kiss, sealing our unspoken bond. "You're magnificent, Paige. If the prince wants you, he'll have to face me and our entire pack."

CHAPTER 10

BLAKE

The moon hangs high in the night sky, casting an ethereal glow over the Ocala pack's territory. It is a restless night, charged with anticipation and apprehension. The very same darkness I felt in the air while training with Paige, is back and is thicker now. Even the wolves can sense it. Ominous quiet settles over the pack as we navigate through the dense forest. The night feels heavy, filled with an unsettling stillness that sends shivers down my spine. The normally lively sounds of nature are hushed as if nature itself holds its breath in anticipation of what is to come.

My warriors move as one, their instincts honed and senses heightened. We proceed with caution, stepping lightly on the forest floor, our movements are synchronized and purposeful. Every now and then, a twig snaps or a rustle breaks the silence, causing us to freeze in our tracks, our ears pricked for any sign of danger.

Beside me, Paige walks with a determination that matches my own. Her presence is a constant source of reassurance and I draw strength from her as she draws strength from me. We share a deep connection, both as mates and as partners in this battle against the encroaching darkness.

As we venture deeper into the heart of the forest, the darkness seems to coagulate, enveloping us like a suffocating shroud. Shadows dance and flicker, playing tricks on our senses and whispers of ancient magic echo through the trees. It is a reminder that our adversary is not to be underestimated.

The wolves of the Ocala pack stay close, their sharp gazes scanning the surroundings, ever watchful for any signs of threat. We move with a primal grace, a unity that comes from years of loyalty, trust and training. Howls in the distance pierce the silence, their mournful chorus a call to arms that echoes through the night. The pack responds, their voices rising in harmony, a powerful declaration of their readiness and resolve.

Suddenly, Jamie bursts through the trees, his eyes wide and alert. His words carry urgency and a touch of fear. "*The Fae-hunter and his army have arrived and the assault has started. This way!*"

My heart clenches at the news, but I push aside any hesitation or doubt. We have prepared for this moment, trained for this very battle. There is no room for fear. I look at Paige and using our telepathic connection I urge her to jump onto my wolf's back. Once she has secured her grip, we sprint forward, keeping pace with the others as we rush toward the impending confrontation.

"How many?" I demand from Jamie as we run, my voice steady despite the turmoil inside me.

His response cuts through the night air, his words heavy with the weight of the impending danger. *"Seventy-five Fae hunters and Fae."*

Adrenaline rushes through my veins, pushing my feet to move faster. We have faced challenges as a pack, but this is a battle that will test our abilities to protect our pack like never before. I am confident in the resilience of our pack and the power of our bond.

With each step, I brace myself for what lies ahead. The moon illuminates our path, guiding us through the darkness as we prepare to confront the Fae-hunter and his army. My pack will stand together, united in purpose and ready to defend our pack, our territory and everything we hold dear.

As we break through a clearing, I stop dead in my tracks, nearly launching my mate from her place on my back. Flickering flames illuminate the battleground, casting an eerie light on the twisted faces of our enemies. Paige climbs down and stands beside me, ready to fight despite my protests. Her determination and unwavering spirit are awe-inspiring, but I cannot bear the thought of her in harm's way.

"Paige, stay close to me," I urged, my voice laced with worry. *"I need you safe."*

She meets my gaze, her eyes brimming with defiance. "I won't hide, Blake. We fight together."

Reluctantly, I give in, knowing that her resolve matches my own. I order two trusted wolves to keep watch over her and they stick by her side at once. As the battle commences, chaos erupts around us.

Sword's clash, claws rip through flesh and magic crackles in the air. It's a dance of violence and survival. Blood stains the ground, mingling with the earth beneath our feet. Losses are suffered on both sides, but our determination remains unyielding.

The scent of fear mingles with that of victory, driving us forward. With each strike, with each roar, I am fueled by the unwavering love for my pack and the fierce protectiveness I feel for Paige. The battle rages on echoing through the night.

Suddenly, a low grumble reverberates through the air and a figure materializes from the shadows, standing several feet away from us. It is the Fae hunter, a malicious smile playing on his lips.

"Ah, the Alpha and his fated mate," he sneers, his voice filled with arrogance. "Such a delightful reunion we're having."

I quickly shift back into my human form and step forward, my body tensed, ready to strike. "You've made a grave mistake by targeting my pack and my mate. You will pay for your actions."

The Fae hunter chuckles darkly, his eyes glinting with a sadistic gleam. "Oh, I think you underestimate me, *Alpha*." He draws out the title, mocking the respect its meaning demands.

Paige's hands tightened into fists, her eyes narrowing with determination. "We don't fear you," she declares, her voice steady. "We will protect our pack at all costs."

The Fae hunter's smile widens, a glimmer of excitement dancing in his eyes. "How touching. But let's see how well you fare against my Faes' magic."

He raises his hand, summoning his Fae allies, motioning for a swirling vortex of dark energy. Shadows twist and coil around him and his Fae, forming a shield of darkness. Without a moment's hesitation, the Fae hurls bolts of malevolent energy toward us.

I dive to the side, narrowly avoiding the attack, while Paige raises her arms, summoning a wall of air to shield us. The energy collides with the barrier, causing the ground to tremble under the impact.

"We need to find a weakness," I shout over the chaos, my mind racing with strategies. "They draw power from the shadows. If we can disrupt that connection..."

Paige nods, her eyes blazing with determination. "Let me try to disrupt that control over the shadows."

As she focuses her energy, the air around us crackles with

anticipation. She stretches out her arms, palms facing the hunter and Fae and channels her power into a concentrated burst. She hurls a fierce gust of wind, tearing through the battlefield, scattering the darkness and forcing the Fae and hunter to fall backward.

With the shield of shadows weakened, I seized the opportunity, launching myself in wolf form at the Fae hunter with a primal roar. Our movements are a blur of fury and skill. Teeth and claws clash with magic, each strike fueled by determination and a deep-seated desire to protect our pack.

Paige joins the fray, her elemental powers adding an extra layer of chaos to the battlefield. Fire engulfs the hunter, burning away his dark defenses, while gusts of wind whip around the Fae, disorienting their movements.

Together we fight as one, our movements in sync and strengthening with each blow delivered. With each strike, we chip away at the Fae hunter and his Fae's magic, leaving them all vulnerable and exposed.

In a final, decisive move, I deliver a powerful blow by my claws to the Fae Hunter's chest and abdomen that send him crashing to the ground. His blood-curdling cry echoes through the trees. Blood gushes from his abdomen and he chokes on it as he tries to speak. As the Fae hunter writhes in pain, his malevolent Fae and their magic severely wanes.

"I told you," I tell him between heaving breaths, back into my human form, "my pack will not let you have her."

He hacks and coughs, the color draining from his ashen

face. The dark energy that protected him totally dissipates, leaving behind only a sense of victory and relief by us, as we watch until the very last breath escapes his lips. Seeing their leader vanquished, the rest of his army, including the Fae, retreats into the woods.

"Let them go," I order my wolves as they attempt to chase after the deserters. "We got the one who counts."

Amidst the chaos, I catch sight of Lupe lying motionless on the blood-soaked ground. Panic surges through me and tears burn in my eyes, threatening to come crashing through. I rush to her side, fearing the worst, but Paige, ever the beacon of hope, reaches Lupe before I do.

"It's okay," she assures me, holding up a hand to keep me at bay. "I can fix this."

I chose to trust her and take a step back as she rests her hands on the wound in Lupe's leg. It is bleeding out fast and I realize whoever attacked her nicked an artery. I pace back and forth, combing my fingers through my hair, as I watch Paige lean over my sister's lifeless body.

With a touch of her hands, Paige invokes her healing magic, covering Lupe's wounds. The energy flows from her fingertips, mending the broken and revitalizing the fading. I watch in awe, my admiration for Paige growing with each passing moment.

What else is she capable of manifesting? What other untapped powers lie dormant within her? These questions swirl in my mind, igniting a thirst for understanding.

"Guess we'll find out together," Paige smirks at me over her shoulder. "What? You forgot I can read your mind now? Better be careful what thoughts you let slip in there."

I grant her a shaky smile, but when Lupe's eyes flutter open, I run to them, embracing them both at once. "Thank you," I whisper into my mate's hair as I kiss the side of her face. "Thank you so much."

Together, we stand on the battlefield, victorious and united. Paige runs from one injured wolf to another until she has saved all that were still capable of being saved. Then she moves on to the hunter's warriors. The kindness in her heart will not let her walk away from the suffering, even if they were once our enemies. As she tends to their wounds, her healing touch brings relief and solace to those who had been caught in the merciless grip of battle.

As the wounded are cared for and the battle subsides, the pack gathers around, their bodies weary but their hearts filled with triumph. The night air, once heavy with foreboding, now carries a sense of relief and renewed hope. We emerged victorious, standing tall.

The moonlight bathes us in its ethereal glow, casting a soft radiance on our battered forms. We take a moment to honor the fallen, paying our respects to those who fought bravely but did not survive. Their sacrifice will not be forgotten and their spirits will forever live on in the hearts of the pack.

CHAPTER II
PAIGE

"Blake, please, take a moment to rest," I implore, my voice laced with concern. "You've done more than any alpha would do. You need to take care of yourself."

The aftermath of the battle hangs heavy in the air, mingling with the scent of blood and the echoes of victory. Blake's determination knows no bounds as he tirelessly works to clean up the devastation left in the wake of the Fae hunter's assault. His steadfast dedication to his pack is both admirable and concerning.

"I'm fine," he grumbles, but even his protests are beginning to wane.

"You've been going nonstop for two days, with little rest and sustenance. You're running on sheer willpower and love for the pack, but you're pushing yourself to the brink of exhaustion."

He looks at me, his eyes reflecting both weariness and determination. "I can't stop, Paige. Not yet. There's still so much to be done and I can't rest until our home is as back to normal as it can be and our fallen pack members are properly laid to rest."

I understand his perspective, his alpha instincts compelling him to provide comfort and closure to his grieving pack. But I also know the toll it is taking on him, both physically and emotionally.

"You need to breathe," Jaime urges him. "I can take things from here while you rest."

Lupe tugs on her brother's arm. "Come on, Blake. Go back to the pack cabin with Paige and at least eat something."

Blake sighs, giving in to their pleas. He looks at me; his exhaustion is evident in the lines etched on his face. "Fine," he concedes, his voice laced with weariness. "But only for a little while. There's still much to be done."

I nod, relieved that he is willing to take a break, even if it's just a temporary one. Together, we make our way back to the cabin, our steps slow and deliberate. The weight of the battle still hangs heavily on our shoulders, but for this moment, we allow ourselves a reprieve.

Inside the cabin, the atmosphere is hushed, contrasting with all the activity outside; the scent of wood and warmth envelopes us, providing a sense of calm. We settle down on the worn couch, our bodies sinking into the familiar comfort it offers. The fire roars in the hearth, casting a warm shadows across the room and I find myself drawn to its gentle dance.

Blake sits beside me, releasing a groan as he relaxes into the cushions. I reach out and take his hand in mine, linking our fingers. The connection between us is palpable, a lifeline that keeps us grounded amid the turmoil.

"Paige," Blake says, his voice filled with gratitude, "I don't know what I would do without you. You've been my rock throughout all of this."

I squeeze his hand gently, my heart swelling with love for this remarkable man. "And you've been mine, Blake. We are in this as partners and as mates, right?"

We sit in comfortable silence for a while, the sparkling fire providing a soothing backdrop. The weariness seeps into my bones and I realize just how drained I am from the battle. I find solace in knowing that we fought with everything we had and we emerged victorious.

Eventually, I break the silence, my voice soft and filled with concern. "Blake, promise me that you'll take care of yourself. The pack needs you, they need their alpha to be clear headed and healthy."

He meets my gaze, the weariness still present in his eyes, but a flicker of determination shines through. "I promise," he whispers, his voice filled with sincerity. "I won't let my exhaustion put the pack at risk. I'll rest and I'll recover."

With that assurance, I lean in and rest my head on his

shoulder, seeking comfort in his presence. The rhythmic rise and fall of his chest soothe my racing thoughts and for a moment, the weight of responsibility feels a little lighter.

"Come on," I take his hand. "Let's get you up to bed."

As we enter his bedroom, I guide Blake to sit on the edge of the bed. I sit behind him and place my hands on his shoulders, massaging them gently, willing the tightness to melt away. "You're carrying the weight of the pack on your shoulders, Blake," I say softly. "But now, it's time to let someone else take care of you."

"I'm just worried about everyone. We lost good wolves out there and it's my responsibility to honor their sacrifice."

"And you will," I assure him. "But right now, you need to recharge. You are not alone in this. We're a pack and we'll take care of each other."

He leans forward, resting his head on my shoulder. "Thank you, Paige," he whispers.

I wrap my arms around him, holding him close.

After a moment of quiet embrace, I guide Blake to lie down on the bed, his tired body sinking into the soft mattress. I remove his boots and socks, then begin unbuttoning his shirt, taking my time with each button. As I peel the fabric away, revealing his strong chest, I cannot help but marvel at the scars and battle-worn muscles that tell the story of his superior fighting skills.

"You're a superb warrior, Blake," I say, my voice filled with admiration. "But even superb warriors need rest."

He gives me a faint smile, his eyes heavy. "I suppose you're right."

With gentle hands, I continue undressing him, removing his shirt and pants until he lies before me, bare and vulnerable. I lean down, pressing a tender kiss against his forehead. "Just close your eyes and let go, Blake. I'm here for you."

His eyes flutter shut and I watch as his body relaxes into the mattress. I crawl up beside him, wrapping my arms around his warm form. We lie there in silence, our breathing syncing in a tranquil rhythm.

As time passes, I feel the weight of the battles we have fought and the victories we've won settle upon me. The intensity of our connection becomes even more apparent and I find myself wanting to share more than just physical intimacy with Blake. I need to know him on a deeper level.

"Blake," I whispered, breaking the silence, "tell me about your childhood. What was it like growing up as an alpha's son?"

He turns his head to face me, his eyes filled with a mix of nostalgia and sadness. "It wasn't easy," he admits, his voice tinged with emotion. "There were expectations placed upon me from an early age; training, responsibilities and the weight of leadership. But my father taught me the importance of balance. He showed me how to lead with compassion, honesty and bravery."

I listen intently, captivated by his words. "And what about love?" I ask softly. "Have you ever been in love before?"

A hint of a smile tugs at the corners of his lips. "No, Paige. I can honestly say that I have never felt a love as deep as what I feel for you. You've opened my heart in ways I didn't know were possible."

My heart swells with warmth and I reach out to brush my fingers against his cheek. "I love you, Blake. With all that I am."

He cups my face in his hands, his gaze filled with tenderness. "And I love you, Paige. You are my everything."

Before I can stop myself, I'm on top of him and our lips collide. His tongue explores my mouth as my fingers take on a life of their own, tracing the muscles of his abdomen. I grind my pelvis into his naked torso, desperate to feel every inch of him inside of me. Blake's hand tangles into my hair and he yanks it back, exposing my neck. He nips at the sensitive skin and I whimper at the way it excites me.

I pull away and slide down, my eyes fixed on his as I glide my tongue down his chest and stomach, gripping the shaft of his manhood in my hand. He moans as I move my hand in rhythm with the movement of his hips. I continue my descent, crawling backward until I can flick the tip of his hardness with my tongue licking up his precum. He growls as I take him into my mouth and his shaft pulses with his heartbeat.

Suddenly, in one swift motion, Blake grabs my body, pulls me up and flips us until he's on top of me. His fingers find my folds and I push against them as they penetrate me. My heart is hammering against my ribcage, my breathing ragged and desperate. Sweat beads Blake's brow, his excitement shown when I arch my back and beg him to take me.

In that moment, we surrender to the depth of our love, and Blake enters me with powerful strokes making sure all of him is in me as our bodies become one again. But this time, our lovemaking is not just a physical release; it's an affirmation of the bond we share. With each touch, each whisper of devotion, we reaffirm our commitment to one another.

As the waves of pleasure wash over us, our bodies find release and our hearts find solace and healing.

As we lay embracing each other, our breaths gradually slowing, I know that this moment of rest is not just about physical rejuvenation. It's about the rekindling of our spirits, replenishing of our love and fortifying ourselves for the battles that may still lay ahead.

CHAPTER 12

BLAKE

The sun begins to set, casting a warm glow over the cabin deck where Paige and I sit together on the swing, wrapped in each other's arms. From this vantage point, we watch the pack's playful pups frolic in front of us, a sight that fills my heart with contentment. With Paige by my side, I feel a sense of completion, as if the missing piece of our pack has finally fallen into place.

Suddenly, Lupe approaches us, hauling a woman forward by the back of the neck.

"Queen Sebille!" Paige is on her feet in an instant and my protective instincts surge to the surface. I tried to step in front of her, but she bolts past me, planting herself in front of the pack of pups in the yard.

"Paige," I call as I run after her, ready to defend her and our pack from any potential threat.

"Alpha," Lupe speaks quickly, full of urgency, "we caught her spying on us from the woods."

Paige's mouth is agape and her head is tilted to the side.

"What is she doing here?" I demand.

"She claims she means no harm," Lupe explains, "But her presence here raises questions that need answers."

I reach Paige's side, my instincts still heightened as I assess the situation. Queen Sebille stands before us, her eyes darting nervously between us and the pack of playful pups. Despite the air of authority she carries, there is a vulnerability in her stance that hints at something more beneath the surface.

Paige's voice cuts through the tension, her tone firm but curious. "Queen Sebille, why have you come to our territory? What brings you here and why were you spying on us?"

Sebille's gaze meets Paige's and there is a flicker of recognition in her eyes. She looks at me and says, "You must be the alpha."

"That's right," I confirm with a sharp nod.

"I'm honest when I say I mean no harm," she says, her voice tinged with a mix of apprehension and desperation. "I came looking for Paige. I received word Prince Beckett sent a hunter after her and I feared the worst."

"Paige is safe. My pack and I have taken care of the Fae hunter and we will deal with Beckett himself if we need to."

"May I address her directly?" The Fae queen locks eyes with Paige, her voice trembling with sincerity. "Paige, my dear, I deeply regret the danger I unknowingly placed you in. I never intended for any harm to come your way."

Paige looks at me briefly, seeking reassurance, before turning her attention back to the Fae queen. "Tell me, Queen Sebille. Did you authorize Prince Beckett's hunt?"

Sebille's eyes widen and she shakes her head vehemently. "No, Paige. I had no knowledge of Beckett's actions. He has grown reckless and power-hungry, and I have lost control over him. I never wanted this for you."

Paige's gaze narrows, her voice steady but cautious. "If you're not in league with Beckett, then why were you spying on us? Why not approach us directly?"

Queen Sebille's shoulders slump and a shadow of shame passes over her features. "I was afraid, Paige. Afraid of how you would react to my sudden appearance. Afraid of the pain it would bring to both of us. I wanted to assess the situation from afar before revealing myself."

Paige's eyes soften. "Your Majesty, I have learned much during this journey. I understand that your actions were driven by the best of intentions. We must move forward and strive for peace between our families."

The Fae queen's eyes filled with tears and her emotions lay bare before us. She reaches out to touch Paige's hand, her voice filled with gratitude. "Paige, my dear, I am grateful for your forgiveness. You have grown into a remarkable young woman, embodying a strength and resilience that few possess."

I step forward, standing beside Paige, projecting both authority and understanding. "Your Majesty, if what you say about Prince Beckett is true, you must know he won't stop. With you as an ally, we can forge a future where our kind can coexist in harmony."

"Yes, of course. I could not agree more."

The Fae queen's eyes shimmer with gratitude as she embraces Paige, the moment resonating with reconciliation and healing. It is a turning point, a step toward mending wounds that have festered for far too long.

As they part, the Fae queen's gaze meets mine. "Alpha Blake, I pledge the allegiance of my clan to you and your pack. We will stand by your side, offering our support and strength in the face of adversity."

I nod, acknowledging her commitment, and I address her with a mixture of gratitude and caution. "Your Majesty, we appreciate your pledge and the trust you place in us. However, I must stress the importance of transparency and open communication moving forward."

"So, no more sneaking around," Paige adds with a giggle.

The Fae queen nods in agreement; her voice filled with determination. "I assure you both. We will be steadfast in our commitment as allies. Our alliance will not only benefit your pack but also the Fae realm as a whole."

Paige locks her arms with the queen, helping her up the steps and leading her into the cabin. "Just wait until you see what I learned to do."

"Not in the cabin," I call to her. "For the love of God, no fire in the cabin."

Did you like this book? Then you'll *LOVE*
The Alpha's Forbidden Panther
Read the blurb below.

An Alpha Werewolf and a Fierce Panther Shifter.
Forbidden.

I am Shuri, a panther shifter, on a search to find the killers of my family.
A feared and agile fighter, I know how to survive on my own.
But I make a mistake and get captured by the Alpha wolf shifter whom I've been tracking.

Then destiny steps in. A new Alpha, Jamie, challenges my jailer, for his pack.
Jamie is gorgeous and makes my body feel things I don't quite understand. But I hate that he takes my revenge from me.

He believes he is only allowed one mate, and his died years ago.
Jamie and I create alliances and prepare for a battle with hunters that are amassing an army, and we grow close.

Our hunter battle seems hopeless, we're so outnumbered.
Our relationship seems doomed, forbidden and against all practices.
My future appears grim and lonely.

Find *The Alpha's Forbidden Panther Here:*
Aamazon.com/dp/B0CQJ1XJ9Y

To read more about Queen Sebille, read
The Queen's Rogue Alpha

**The Queen of the Fae and a Rogue Alpha Wolf Shifter—
married?
Who knew!!**

I am Queen Sebille, the Queen of the Fae.
I aligned with Wolf Shifter Packs to save my Realm.
My council isn't pleased with that wolf alliance and now Fae
are losing their magic.

The council's answer to everything is for me to marry, soon!
I don't need a mate, but if I must, I'll find my own mate, not
one selected by the council.

***

I am Aidan, a rogue Alpha wolf shifter.
My wolf pack was wiped out by hunters.
In seeking revenge, I secretly jumped into the battle between
aligned wolf packs with Fae warriors and an army of hunters.

Alone again, I'm trying to decide whether to join a wolf pack or to move on.

But a one-night stand with a beautiful, enchanting Fae Queen turns into a marriage proposal.

Find *The Queen's Rogue Alpha Here:*

Amazon.com/dp/B0CQJ38ZGS

ALSO BY SHERYL NORBUT

ALPHA SHIFTER ROMANCES

The Alpha's Rejected Fae — *A reader magnet that you can get for free by signing up for my author newsletter here:* **https://BookHip. com/ZVHGDXB**

- ***Alpha's Forbidden Panther*** — https://www.a-mazon.com/dp/B0CQJ1XJ9Y
- ***The Queen's Rogue Alpha*** — https://www.a-mazon.com/dp/B0CQJ38ZGS

ABOUT THE AUTHOR

Sheryl is an avid reader and author of paranormal romance with mystery novels. She lives in the Southeast U.S. but loves traveling. She especially likes to visit Scotland whenever she has a chance. Her novels will always have adventure, intrigue, or mystery coupled with romance as the main players go on their journeys together. And every book will have a happy ending, for the main characters anyway.

You may contact her here at:

Sherylnorbut1@gmail.com

Printed in Great Britain
by Amazon